D1276851

Inspired by **A. A. MILNE**

Winnie-the-Pooh's
1·2·3

With illustrations by

ERNEST H. SHEPARD

Anytime Books

NEW YORK

Published in the United States by Anytime Books,
an imprint of Penguin USA
375 Hudson Street
New York, New York 10014

Printed in Hong Kong

one balloon

two umbrellas

three bells

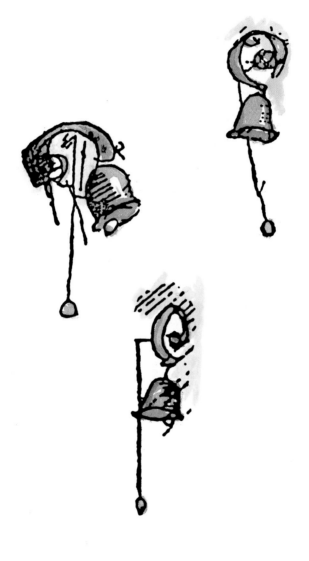

four candles

five beetles

six boots

seven baskets

eight birds

nine dandelions

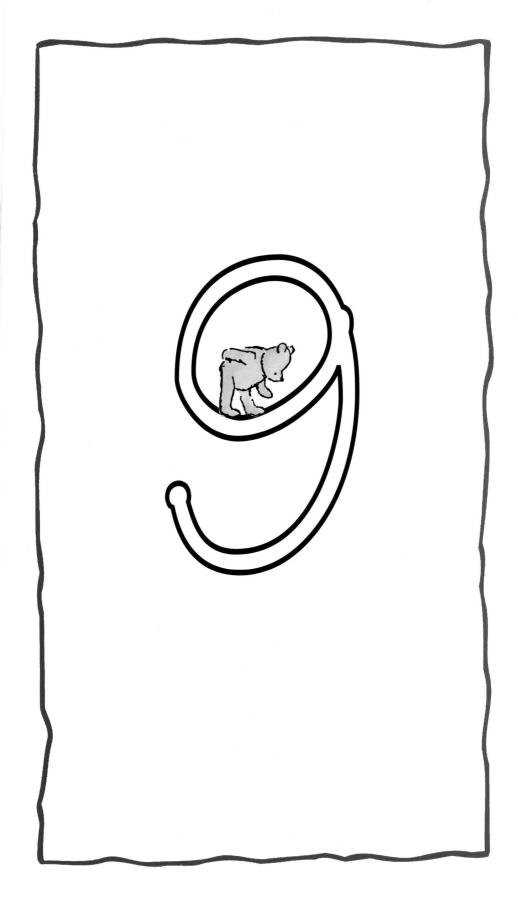

ten honey pots

eleven trees

twelve bees

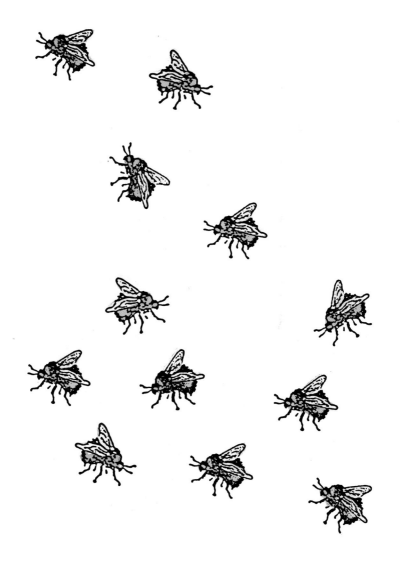